A Chance to Shine

by Jill Atkins and Beatriz Castro

FRANKLIN WATTS
LONDON•SYDNEY

A Chance to Shine

Contents

Chapter 1

In Training

Crack! The starter's gun made Lily jump. Up and away she raced, her feet pounding along the track. Perhaps she would reach the finish line first!

But no, it was not to be. It never was. Almost at once, the other runners began edging ahead on either side, and by the time she reached the end of the race, Lily was last. She knelt by the side of the track, hot and panting. She had a stitch in her side and it hurt.

Abe came over to her. "Well done, little sister," he beamed.

"I was rubbish!" snapped Lily, holding back the tears.

Abe smiled. "OK, OK, I was only trying to ..."

"... cheer me up? Yeah, I know," muttered Lily. "Sorry."

"Anyway, it was only a practice."

"Not that I'll do any better next time," Lily sighed. "I hate
coming here."

It was different for Abe. Lily knew he loved athletics club.

"Molly and Sita wanted me to go shopping with them
this evening," she sighed. "But I knew Mum and Dad
wouldn't let me miss a practice session."

Abe linked arms with Lily. "Yeah. It's rotten for you.
I know you don't enjoy it like I do. Come on. Dad will
be waiting."

They left the track.

Lily looked up at Abe. He was so tall now he was fifteen. He had always been athletic. He could run really fast and could jump a long way. He was the exact opposite of her. She was no good at athletics.

Just then, Jackie, their coach, came up to them.

"Great show, Abe," she gushed. "You'll be a world champion one day!"

Abe had excelled in practice, as usual. He had won the 100 metres and out-jumped – by miles – all the other kids in the long jump and triple jump. But he was always modest about it. That was what made Lily so fond of him.

Dad was sitting in the car. "Well, Abe?" he asked.

"Did you win?"

"Yeah," Abe admitted quietly.

"Marvellous! You really shine on the field." Then Dad chuckled. "You take after your parents, of course!"

Lily sat in the car and stared out the window, thinking. Athletics seemed to be all Dad cared about. She knew why it was so important to him. In his youth, he had been National Triple Jump Champion. Mum, too, had won hundreds of track medals.

"And how did you get on, Lily?" Dad looked at her in the rear-view mirror. She shrugged.

"Not to worry," he said. "Keep practising."

That was all he ever said. She was sick of practising.

As soon as they arrived home, Lily ran up to her room and called Molly.

Molly's diary

Wednesday 5th June

Had a great time shopping today, but it would have been so much more fun if Lily had been there. Just spoke to her on the phone. She sounded OK to begin with then got really upset when I mentioned training.

When I asked her why she doesn't tell her parents, she said she can't. She doesn't want to let them down because they desperately want her to shine on the athletics track like her brother.

I got cross with her then. But when I realised how fed up she was, I tried to make up for that by inviting her to a sleepover with me and Sita next Saturday. But that made things worse. Would you believe it? She's got a race meet that evening so she can't come. She hung up on me like she was upset. I could tell she was on the verge of tears.

I feel so sorry for her. She's not the world's greatest athlete and I know she really hates all this training stuff and dreads the races. But she bugs me, too! I wish she'd stand up to her parents. Can't they see how unhappy she is? And now she can't come to our sleepover. I'd make a right stink if my parents were like that. I wish she would!

8

Chapter 2

Abe's Progress

"Good results today?" Mum asked as she served up dinner.

"Yeah, slightly better than last time," Abe said. "The track felt really smooth so I was able to cut a fraction of a second off my best time."

Date	100 metres	Long Jump	Triple Jump	
28th May	12:05 seconds	7 m 64 cm	15 m 05 cm	Practice
5th June	12:01 seconds	7 m 71 cm	15 m 34 cm	Practice
8th June				Competition

"That's brilliant," said Mum, smiling. "It shows you're on form. How about your jumps?"

"Both good, thanks. My lift-offs were spot on. I can't wait for the competition at the weekend."

Mum gave him a hug. "I'm so proud of you, Abe."

Mum and Dad were extremely supportive, but he wished Mum didn't treat him so much like a superstar. He was only doing something he loved.

Abe smiled, looking back at his chart. It was so rewarding to see how he was improving all the time. But then he frowned as he remembered Lily. His success didn't help her, he knew. She had always been such fun – full of laughter and jokes, but lately she had become much quieter.

Chapter 3
Audition!

At school the next morning, Lily spotted a large notice

pasted on the board in the entrance hall.

"Wow! I'm going for that!" she exclaimed to her friends.

"I've always wanted to be in a play. What about you lot?"

"Sounds good," Sita and Molly agreed.

"I'm in," said George.

All that morning, Lily found it hard to concentrate on her lessons. She daydreamed during maths, imagining herself in the starring role. Several times, her teacher reminded her to get on with her work.

At last, it was lunchtime. She felt too excited to eat her packed lunch, and by 12.45 she couldn't wait another second. She hurried to the hall, followed by Molly and Sita. Quite a lot of boys and girls were already there. Lily swallowed hard. She hadn't expected there would be so much competition. At one o'clock, Mr Dabrowski came into the hall. He smiled to see so many interested faces.

"Thanks for coming, everyone," he began, handing round a sheet of paper for them to sign up. "I bet you've been wondering which play we're going to do this year." Everyone nodded. "Well, it's a new play I've written myself, called *The Strange Adventures of Sally Malone*. It's a comedy. To audition, I want you to imagine you're a mischievous old woman who can perform tricks. Let's see what you can do." A few boys started to grumble and shake their heads. "That includes you, lads," smiled Mr Dabrowski. "I'm looking for the best person for each part."

Lily watched the other children as they tried to portray the woman Mr Dabrowski had described. Most of them showed a bent, doddery little person, but Lily decided her character would be different. Not all older people were bent and doddery! Finally, it was her turn.

She strutted about the stage, turning a cartwheel, wagging her finger at Mr Dabrowski and throwing herself into the part. By the end of her performance, everyone was laughing, including Mr Dabrowski. "That was great, Lily," he shouted across the noise. "Right everyone. Thank you all for coming. You've all done really well. There are lots of parts in the play. I reckon it's fair to say you'll all be in it, if you'd like to be. I'll let you know ... same time tomorrow."

Lily desperately wanted the main part in the play, but would her performance fit with what Mr Dabrowski wanted?
"You were brilliant!" Molly chuckled as they left the hall.
"I bet you get the part."
Lily crossed her fingers and made a wish.

After school, Lily rushed home.

"Guess what! I had an audition for the school play today," she said, bursting into the kitchen where Mum was doing the washing. She smiled at Lily.

"I'll know tomorrow if I got the part," Lily said, excitedly.

"That's nice," her mum replied as she carried the washing out. Lily went upstairs. She was sure her mum hadn't heard a word she'd said.

"And even if she had," thought Lily, "would she be interested?"

Chapter 4
Getting the Part

The morning lessons dragged. But at last, it was one o'clock

and Lily joined the others in the hall. She felt a little sick.

"Right," said Mr Dabrowski, hurrying over to them.

"I have an announcement: the person I've chosen to play

the part of Sally Malone is ..." Lily held her breath.

"... Lily!"

Lily's eyes popped open. "Me? Really?"

Molly gave her a hug and George cheered.

"I told you," Molly whispered. Lily didn't know what to say.

"Well, are you pleased?" laughed Mr Dabrowski.

"Wow! Yes, Sir! Pleased? Wow! Yes! Thank you, Sir!"

"It will be a lot of work," Mr Dabrowski told her.

"Lots of lines to learn and rehearsals. Still OK?"

"Definitely!"

Lily couldn't believe her luck. She waited, shaking slightly with excitement, while Mr Dabrowski allocated the other parts. Molly and Sita were pleased with the parts they were given. George cheered loudly and punched the air when he was given an important role.

"OK, learn what you can this weekend," said Mr Dabrowski. "First rehearsal is on Wednesday after school."

Lily peeped at the typed pages before thrusting them in her school bag. Mr Dabrowski was right. It did mean hard work. There seemed to be thousands of words to learn. Still, she could manage that. She knew she could.

Lily and Molly talked about the play as they walked home after school that afternoon. But just as they approached her house, Lily suddenly stopped.

"What's up?" asked Molly.

"I've just realised something terrible," said Lily.

"Wednesday's play rehearsal after school ... I was so excited I completely forgot ... it's athletics training."

Lily went straight to find Abe. "I've got a problem," she said.

"Hey, Sis. What's up?" he said, looking up from the book he was reading in the lounge. Lily sat down beside him.

"I've been given the leading role in our school play."

"Yay! So why is that a problem?"

"The first rehearsal is on Wednesday after school."

"So?" said Abe, puzzled.

"It's athletics."

"Ah! Do Mum and Dad know?"

Lily shook her head. "I'm dreading telling them."

Abe was silent for a few minutes, then he said,

"Well, we'd better go and tell Mum."

"We? Will you come with me?"

"Of course! What are big brothers for? Leave it to me. I'll persuade her."

Molly's diary

Wednesday 7th June

I'm so pleased Lily got that part today. I knew she would. She deserves it. She's a natural. The rest of us hadn't even thought of making the character a lively old lady.

But poor Lily, not daring to tell her mum she'll have to miss athletics training. I wonder if she has managed it though. I just hope her parents will soon realise how talented she is!

***

Chapter 5

Thanks to Abe

Abe and Lily went into the kitchen together.

Mum looked up from her laptop. "Hello," she said.

"Had a good day?"

"Yes, thanks," said Lily nervously. "Mum ... you remember

I told you about the auditions yesterday?"

"Yes?"

"Well," Lily continued, "I got the part."

"That's great."

"Our first rehearsal is on Wednesday after school so ..." Lily paused, anxious about her mum's reaction, "... I'll have to skip athletics training."

Mum frowned. "Your athletics training must come first if you want to be a top athlete."

"Actually, Mum, she doesn't," Abe interrupted.

"She didn't want to tell you and Dad because athletics is so important to you both. She has been trying to please you, but I have seen how unhappy she has been."

"Well, Lily's always been a bit of an actress," Mum began, "but ..."

Abe sat down next to Mum. "And I think doing this play is as important to Lily as athletics is to me," he said.

Lily nodded. "Please, Mum."

Saturday was the race meeting. It was a miserable day for Lily. She ran in the second heat of the 60 metres and came last. But even though her racing was over for the day, Mum and Dad insisted she stay at the track. It was so boring, although she watched Abe and cheered him on in each of his events. Lily wished she had brought her play script with her. She had learned the lines of the first scene, but there was so much more to learn. She was nervous, but looking forward to the first rehearsal.

As they walked away from the track at the end of the meet, Mum put her arm round Abe's shoulders. "You were fantastic," she said. "Well done. I'm so proud of you." Abe rolled his eyes at Lily.

Abe hurried to the kitchen as soon as they arrived home. Mum and Dad watched him fill in his latest figures.

Dad patted Abe on the back.

"You're improving," he laughed. "Just like your dad, eh?"

Abe didn't know what to say. He was pleased with each improvement, but knew it must be hard for Lily, hearing Mum and Dad praising him all the time.

Molly's diary

Wednesday 12th June

Lily is amazing! How did she manage to learn all those lines? The rest of us had to rely on our scripts at the rehearsal today. And she got the character of Sally Malone absolutely perfectly. Mr Dabrowski said so. Lily is very modest about it. I hope her parents allow her to go on with it. If I were her, I'd rebel!

Chapter 6
Important Dates

Mr Dabrowski insisted that they rehearse every lunchtime over the next two weeks.

"This is a real chance for you all to shine," he said firmly. "The play is coming on marvellously!"

Lily loved every moment of rehearsals. She was really into her part, thinking and acting like Sally Malone.

"Hey, Lily!" said Abe one afternoon. "You're really enjoying this, aren't you? I can't wait to see you in action!"

But when Lily came home with the school letter showing the dates of the performances, Abe groaned.

"That's so unfair!" he exclaimed. "Those are the exact dates of my trials for the national team. I was so looking forward to your play, but now I won't be able to come!"

Lily hugged him. "Not to worry," she mumbled, trying to hide her disappointment.

"I feel really bad about it," said Abe.

Lily shrugged. "Next time."

Lily gave the school letter to her mum.

"It's an invitation to the play," she said. "Look, there's a form to fill in at the bottom. How many tickets do you want?"

Mum frowned and reached for her diary. "Ah!" she said as she found the page. "Abe's trials are on those days. What a pity, Lily. We won't be able to come to your play."

Lily shut herself in her room. She lay on her bed and stared at the ceiling, feeling hurt and rejected.

Just then, her phone vibrated.

Molly's diary

Friday 28th June

I just called Lily. I said I bet she's excited about the play because I certainly am. I'm really pleased that my mum and dad and gran and grandad all want to come. Then I had a massive shock. Lily told me her parents aren't coming. That's unbelievable! Even worse, it's because it's Abe's national trials on the same dates.

I shrieked when she told me. I must have deafened her. I told her it was criminal and she admitted she was a bit upset. A bit? I should think so. I asked her straight – why is it always Abe, Abe, Abe with them? But she insisted it wasn't his fault. Apparently, he feels bad about it. Anyway, she said she'd see me tomorrow and hung up.

Chapter 7

A Chance to Shine

Lily stood at the front of the stage, in the centre of a long line of performers. She beamed as they all bowed. The audience clapped and cheered. Lily felt exhilarated. Both performances had gone brilliantly. Of course, she had been terrified beforehand, with butterflies in her stomach, but as soon as she had stepped on the stage, they had disappeared.

All the cast had acted so well, and now Mr Dabrowski, standing at the side of the stage, was cheering the loudest.

Later, as they left the hall, Molly's gran took Lily's arm. "You're a star, Lily. You really are!" she said. Glowing from all the praise, Lily sat in the back of Molly's parents' car as they drove home. She had had such a fantastic experience, but she couldn't help thinking of the one thing that hadn't been perfect. Neither her parents nor Abe had been there to watch her.

Molly's diary

Friday 12th July

I am so mad! Surely Lily's parents could have missed Abe's sport just this once. Or maybe, just one of them could have come to the play. They missed a treat! They don't seem to realise what a talented person Lily is.

27

The moment Lily walked into the house, Dad grabbed her.

"He did it!" he cheered. "Our Abe made the National Youth Team! How about that?"

"Yes," said Mum. "He broke all his own records! Aren't you proud of your brother, Lily?"

"He knows I am," Lily replied, lifting her hand to high-five Abe. "That's fantastic news!"

Abe grinned. "How did the play go?" he asked.

"Well, thanks."

A week later, Lily had some terrific news – the play had been so popular they were going to perform it one more time.

"That's fantastic," said Mum. "We did feel bad, you know, about not coming before. We'll make sure we're there this time."

On Saturday evening, Lily's parents and Abe hurried

to school to watch Lily in the extra performance of

The Strange Adventures of Sally Malone.

"What a star!" laughed Dad when it was over.

"You really shine, Lily! That was brilliant!" laughed Mum.

"Aren't you proud of your sister, Abe?"

Abe gave Lily a hug. "She knows I am," he said.

Things to think about

1. How does Lily feel about her athletics training?
2. Describe the relationship between Lily and her brother, and Lily and her parents.
3. Molly keeps a diary of her side of Lily's events. Do you agree with Molly's point of view – why / why not?
4. How does Lily feel after her performance is over?
5. How does the teacher, Mr Dabrowski, help Lily?

Write it yourself

This book explores different relationships in a family and different points of view on a situation. Now try writing your own, expressing the different viewpoints of your characters. Plan your story before you begin to write it.

Start off with a story map:

- a beginning to introduce the characters and where and when your story is set (the setting);
- a problem that the main characters will need to fix in the story;
- an ending where the problems are resolved.

Get writing! Try to include a range of different writing styles in your story to express different viewpoints such as newspaper reports, interviews, diary entries, and so on. Think about which methods are most persuasive in conveying a certain point of view.

Notes for parents and carers

Independent reading
The aim of independent reading is to read this book with ease. This series is designed to provide an opportunity for your child to read for pleasure and enjoyment. These notes are written for you to help your child make the most of this book.

About the book
Lily's parents want her to join her older brother Abe and become a star on the athletics track. But Lily does not enjoy athletics at all. When she auditions for a school play, she lands the main part and discovers her true talent lies on the stage, not the track.

Before reading
Ask your child why they have selected this book. Look at the title and blurb together. What do they think it will be about? Do they think they will like it?

During reading
Encourage your child to read independently. If they get stuck on a longer word, remind them that they can find syllable chunks that can be sounded out from left to right. They can also read on in the sentence and think about what would make sense.

After reading
Support comprehension by talking about the story. What happened?
Then help your child think about the messages in the book that go beyond the story, using the questions on the page opposite. Give your child a chance to respond to the story, asking:
Did you enjoy the story and why? Who was your favourite character?
What was your favourite part? What did you expect to happen at the end?

Franklin Watts
First published in Great Britain in 2019
by The Watts Publishing Group

Copyright © The Watts Publishing Group 2019
All rights reserved.

Series Editors: Jackie Hamley, Melanie Palmer and Grace Glendinning
Series Advisors: Dr Sue Bodman and Glen Franklin
Series Designer: Peter Scoulding

A CIP catalogue record for this book is
available from the British Library.

ISBN 978 1 4451 6545 5 (hbk)
ISBN 978 1 4451 6546 2 (pbk)
ISBN 978 1 4451 7035 0 (library ebook)

Printed in China

Franklin Watts
An imprint of
Hachette Children's Group
Part of The Watts Publishing Group
Carmelite House
50 Victoria Embankment
London EC4Y 0DZ

An Hachette UK Company
www.hachette.co.uk

www.franklinwatts.co.uk